It's Hanukkah Time!

Latifa Berry Kropf

photographs by Tod Cohen

KAR-BEN
PUBLISHING

Hugs to the children in this book who did their very best and sometimes had to do it over and over again. Thanks to Congregation Beth Israel's preschool staff who graciously let us disrupt, reorganize, and take over their classrooms . . . to all the grandparents, especially Roger, whose presence added warmth and sweetness to this book . . . to my family and friends who helped eat all the sufganiyot I made while perfecting the recipe.

To all children everywhere. May they always have full tummies and warm beds, joyful holidays, and people who love them.   L.B.K.

To my grandmother, Rose Cohen, and her sister, Celia Horowitz, who always planned the family Hanukkah parties when I was a child.   T.C.

About Hanukkah:
Hanukkah is an eight-day Festival of Lights that celebrates the victory of the Maccabees over the mighty armies of the Syrian king Antiochus. When they restored the Holy Temple in Jerusalem, the Maccabees found one jug of pure oil, enough to keep the menorah burning for just one day. But a miracle happened and the oil burned for eight days. On each night of the holiday, we add an additional candle to the menorah, exchange gifts, play dreidel, and eat fried latkes and sufganiyot to remember this victory for religious freedom.

Text copyright © 2004 by Latifa Berry Kropf
Photos copyright © 2004 by Tod Cohen

Kar-Ben Publishing, Inc.
A division of Lerner Publishing Group
241 First Avenue North
Minneapolis, MN 55401 U.S.A.
800-4-KARBEN

Website address: www.karben.com

Library of Congress Cataloging-in-Publication Data

Kropf, Latifa Berry.
    It's Hanukkah time! / by Latifa Berry Kropf ; photographs by Tod Cohen.
        p.   cm.
    Summary: Preschoolers invite their grandparents to a Hanukkah party and celebrate by lighting the menorah, playing dreidel, making sufganiyot, and telling the story of the Maccabees. Includes facts about Hanukkah and a recipe for sufganiyot.
    ISBN: 1–58013–120–4 (lib. bdg. : alk. paper)
    [1. Hanukkah—Fiction. 2. Parties—Fiction. 3. Grandparents—Fiction.] I.Title: It is Hanukkah time!. II. Cohen, Tod, ill. III. Title.
PZ7.K9229It 2004
[E]—dc22   2003026443

Manufactured in the United States of America
2 3 4 5 6 7 – JR – 10 09 08 07 06 05

GLOSSARY:
Hanukkah: Festival of Lights; the word means *dedication*

Maccabees: A small band of Jewish patriots led by Judah Maccabee

Hanukkah Menorah: Candleholder with room for eight candles and a *shamash* (helper candle used to light the others); the Hebrew word is *hanukkiyah*

Dreidel: Spinning top used to play a holiday game; the letters on the dreidel remind us of the miracle of Hanukkah

Sufganiyot: Donuts traditionally eaten on Hanukkah

Winter is here, and it's getting dark early.
It's almost time to light Hanukkah candles.

We're having a Hanukkah party
for our grandparents. Suzie and Michael
are coloring their dreidel invitations.

Gabe is mailing his invitation.
Won't his grandma be surprised!

We're making picture frames
for our grandparents.

Talia is wrapping her gift.

David and Jennie are hanging sparkly
stars on the wall.

We are ready to clean our classroom,
just like the Maccabees cleaned the Temple.

Henry and his friends are mixing
the batter for *sufganiyot**.

*donuts

After our teacher fries them in oil,
they cool on paper towels.

When the donuts are cool,
we roll them in cinnamon and sugar.

Hooray! Our guests have arrived.

It's time to light four candles for the fourth night of Hanukkah. Rabbi Dan leads us in the blessings.

We're pretending that we're Hanukkah candles.

Sari and her grandpa are playing
a game of dreidel.

It's fun to spin like dreidels.

Joseph's grandfather reads us
a story about Hanukkah.

Talia's grandma is happy to receive her present.

Grandma and Grandpa like to
dance the hora with us.

Who's hungry? Here are the sufganiyot.
They taste yummy.

We end our party with
our favorite Hanukkah songs.

Sufganiyot (Donuts)

Batter:
2 c. flour
½ c. sugar
1 Tbsp. baking powder
¼ c. oil
¾ c. milk
1 egg

½ tsp. salt
oil for deep-frying

Topping:
4 tsp. cinnamon
¾ c. sugar

Mix all of the batter ingredients together in large bowl. Heat cooking oil in deep fryer to 365°F. You can also use a wok or deep frying pan.* Carefully drop batter by spoonfuls into hot oil. Fry for 3 to 5 minutes until brown, turning with a slotted spoon. Remove from oil and drain on paper towels. Mix cinnamon and sugar. When cool enough to touch, roll in cinnamon/sugar mixture.

*Make sure an adult does the deep-frying.

WHY SUFGANIYOT?

Like the traditional potato latkes, sufganiyot are fried in oil and remind us of the miracle of the oil in the Temple. They are the favorite Hanukkah treat in Israel, easy to make, and enjoyed by most young children.

CANDLE BLESSINGS

בָּרוּךְ אַתָּה יְיָ אֱלֹהֵינוּ מֶלֶךְ הָעוֹלָם,
אֲשֶׁר קִדְּשָׁנוּ בְּמִצְוֹתָיו וְצִוָּנוּ לְהַדְלִיק נֵר שֶׁל חֲנֻכָּה.

Baruch Atah Adonai Eloheinu Melech ha'olam,
Asher kid'shanu b'mitzvotav v'tzivanu l'hadlik ner shel Hanukkah.

Blessed are You, Our God, Ruler of the world, who has made us holy
and given us the mitzvah of lighting the Hanukkah candles.

בָּרוּךְ אַתָּה יְיָ אֱלֹהֵינוּ מֶלֶךְ הָעוֹלָם,
שֶׁעָשָׂה נִסִּם לַאֲבוֹתֵינוּ בַּיָּמִים הָהֵם בַּזְּמַן הַזֶּה.

Baruch Atah Adonai Eloheinu Melech ha'olam,
She'asah nisim la'avoteinu bayamim hahem, bazeman hazeh.

Blessed are You, Our God, Ruler of the world, for the miracles
which you performed for our ancestors in those days.

On the first night we add this blessing:

בָּרוּךְ אַתָּה יְיָ אֱלֹהֵינוּ מֶלֶךְ הָעוֹלָם,
שֶׁהֶחֱיָנוּ וְקִיְּמָנוּ וְהִגִּיעָנוּ לַזְּמַן הַזֶּה.

Baruch Atah Adonai Eloheinu Melech ha'olam,
Shehecheyanu, vekiy'manu v'higiyanu laz'man hazeh.

Blessed are You, Our God, Ruler of the world, who has kept us
alive and brought us together to celebrate this special time.